Stand Tough

By

William F. Martin

ISBN: 1-4033-0340-1 (softcover)
ISBN: 1-4033-0339-8 (ebook)

This book is printed on acid free paper.

1stBooks - rev. 03/13/02

Chapter 1.

As Clint pulled his mount to a slow weary halt, the land seemed to fall away from his position on the edge of a high ridge. The land below turned from the beige color around him to a deep green in the distant valley. The hint of green reminded him that he and his horse had been long without water. If someone were to look right into his face, though, they would not have seen a sign of thirst or emotion. His last few years had conditioned him to complete self-control. The blue-gray steel eyes had a hard look about them, but it was more a look of determination than hatred. There were even faint lines of kindness that could be nurtured to grow if treated right.

Clint Mason was a man with a purpose, but the urgency was not so acute. It had been only six weeks ago, late February, that an old, old letter from his brother had finally caught up to him. Or rather, he had finally bumped into it at a post office bulletin board in a feed and grocery store in Abilene. The letter was five years old, nearly faded away and forgotten by everyone. Even the store clerk, who also handled the mail, had probably stopped looking at this faded letter. It was not unusual to see letters posted like that for months and sometimes years.

1

When had he last seen his brother Brad? Must have been almost ten years ago. Clint had said he was headed to Abilene as he was leaving Crossbow. He had told Brad to contact him through the general store in Abilene under the initials C.M. Their parting had been quick and sad. Although these two brothers were as different as night and day, there had always been a bond of closeness and understanding that no one could come between. Clint could not even remember a single fight between them.

It was getting dark, the green valley in the distance was turning a deep purple, then almost black. The chilly air of late March cut right through the range-worn clothes that made up Clint's wardrobe. These clothes were by choice of comfort and disguise. Money had not been a problem. Cool nerve and quick mind had provided ample funds from the rich, flashy, and dumb that chose to play poker in western towns.

Survival was also learned not at cards but due to cards. Clint's skill was often interpreted as too good for luck, thus he was forced to defend his life too many times. It was not that he couldn't handle the cards to his advantage, but there just wasn't any need to resort to that if you had a feeling of every card, could read faces like a mirror and calculated the odds with mathematical skills unknown in the west.

The west played host to many human types. The arrogant, bully gunslinger was seen over and over. Each town seemed to have at least one. Then there were the roving professionals who hired out their gun skill to the highest pay. It was getting so Clint could classify the man by his look, walk, hardware and horse at a single glance. It may have been his knowledge of gunfighter appearances that aided Clint from looking like or being identified with that group. Have no doubt about it, no matter how good and fast you are, there will eventually be someone better. Clint knew his speed was as good or better than anyone he had seen, but why take a chance? Why not use your mind and skills to put the odds in your favor?

The worn cowboy look and his slow, even motion was usually interpreted as the appearance of an ordinary cowboy. Only the most experienced professionals had on occasion seen through that mask into those eyes. Those few times when Clint had been unable to avoid confrontation with these well-known professionals he had gained a hint of his own skill and cunning.

A rock ledge was off to the right, enough off the trail for privacy. The overhang was perhaps twenty feet, plenty of room for him and his horse. It looked like rain, which at this elevation could turn to snow or sleet this time of year. The space was much larger than expected with evidence of digging long ago.

Chapter 2.

Clint unsaddled the roan and only after giving the horse a thorough rubdown with dry grass did he allow himself to tend to his own needs.

The roan stallion grazed nearby, without bridle or rope. The relationship between this horse and man was one of complete trust and friendship. This was understandable recounting how the two had met a little over two years ago. The roan had been trapped in a blind canyon, cornered by a dozen wild dogs. He had gotten a stone lodged into one hoof and had come up lame.

The dog packs just wait for a stray or lame animal, then they move in. The dogs take turns racing in, ripping, tearing and biting to inflict whatever damage they can. Experience has taught them how to wear down the animal. Even the strongest of horses can be downed by a vicious pack.

Clint had heard the dogs for over an hour before he reached the rim of the canyon. At first sight he thought the horse was dead. Only two dogs were still able to cause damage and they were circling the downed horse. The other dogs lay in various parts of the canyon, bruised and immobile. Clint watched for

4

the longest time, not knowing why the dogs didn't move in on the feast for which they had sacrificed so much. Finally, one of the two remaining dogs got up the courage to take a bite. The horse, in one final kick, while lying on its side, smashed the mongrel's head.

The effort left the horse with little strength and Clint could hear the deep rattle of the horse's final breathing. The one remaining dog lay down just out of the horse's circle of reach waiting for the horse to bleed to death. Clint's admiration for the roan had been developed right then. Never had he seen such a heart and power in a horse before. Clint couldn't let that wild mongrel win a battle by cowardly waiting for the horse to bleed to death. A rifle shot in the dirt just in front of the dog proved how cowardly he was. The large mongrel let out, without looking back for his feast or his pack mates that lay wasted after their thwarted efforts to kill this once beautiful horse.

After finishing off several of the broken and battered dogs, Clint decided to make the downed horse as comfortable as possible. A mud pack made of the horse's blood and desert dust, mixed with the little remaining water in his canteen, was all that could be done. The horse was too weak to resist. Its eyes, after those first few gentle pats of mud, shone with real relief and the horse settled into a deep, troubled sleep.

Clint kept watch all night to keep the wild dogs and coyotes away. He also built a large fire to keep the horse warmed from the cold desert night. There was little hope. Such struggles for life by person or animal in their dying moment should be appreciated and rewarded.

Clint's mare, a strong Morgan in her glory days, stood by throughout this ordeal as if understanding. This man had a way with animals that captured their never dying loyalty and encouraged them to give their best. The Morgan mare had run its heart out saving Clint's life over the years, but you could tell that the loyalty to the man was stronger than ever.

As the sun started to rise and the warm rays beat down on the man that had held vigil all night, exhaustion gave way to sleep. Clint had a fleeting dream of offspring between this courageous stallion and the loyal Morgan mare. The combined traits of each could make magnificent animals with power, endurance, heart, courage and loyalty.

The mare was stomping around very nervously. Could that be what had woken Clint? No, there was something else wrong. Sleep cleared from his head in a second and his eyes watched the mare's ears. Something upstream. Now he heard it. It was a washout roaring down the canyon. It had rained during the night up in the mountains and now a killer wall of rock, mud, logs and water was racing toward them.

Clint saw the head of the stallion raise, his torn muscles flex, but he was unable to rise. Quickly, Clint threw a rope over the stallion's head and, without time to saddle or bridle the mare, he jumped on her back and wrapped the rope as far down onto the mare's neck and shoulders as possible. The roar of the washout became almost deafening now. Clint knew they only had seconds to make the bank. The mare, almost pulling the stallion along the ground, was not going to make it at this rate. Clint jumped off the mare. He ran back to the stallion and stood on his front legs, causing them to dig into the soft, sandy streambed. As if by magic, the stallion was pulled onto its feet. The three of them rushed to the safety of the bank and were shielded by some cottonwood stumps and half-dead trees. Within thirty-five minutes the crest had passed and a bond between the three had been sealed forever.

Chapter 3.

Clint worked hurriedly around the face of the overhang to form a water catch. Some old barrows had been left in the dug out, almost cave-like opening. Even before the water catch was complete the rain was coming down hard. The roan stallion was enjoying the rain, even though it was almost cold enough to be sleet. After catching two barrows of water, Clint gathered some dry wood from the back of the cave and got a good warm fire going. He built it back into the opening far enough to avoid sighting by any passers-by and dry enough so the fire hardly put out any smoke at all.

After a good grazing around the hillside, the roan returned to the shelter for the warmth and the companionship of his master and friend. As Clint rubbed the horse down again, he marveled at the strength and power of this horse. Although the scarred body looked to the naive like a run-down old plow horse, that outer appearance was as deceiving for the horse as the worn clothes were for the man.

Clint drank heavily of the cold rainwater because the two of them had survived the last three days on a single canteen of water. They had also lost the Morgan mare a couple of days ago to a treacherous rock slide.

Both Clint and the roan stallion felt the loss and missed their companion.

Clint had a meal of dry, tough, but tasty beef jerky and a slow aromatic smoke of his special St. Louis blend pipe tobacco. Now to plan his strategy for helping Brad, if his brother was still alive. One thing for sure, Brad would never have asked him to risk returning to Crossbow unless all other options had been tried. A fear welled up in Clint's throat, afraid to say it, but knowing that help five years late may be like no help at all. Clint had come as quickly as he had gotten the letter. Why hadn't he checked in Abilene before? He had done so the first few years after he had hurriedly left Crossbow. There were a thousand questions in his mind. The letter had been brief, saying only that Captain Carl Hudson had turned out to be powerful and now owned the majority of the choice land in the county, with most of it obtained through foreclosures on other ranch families. Brad's bank was trying to hold off Captain Hudson's intrusion into his bank, but the community lenders were looking to Hudson as a financial savior and civic leader. Brad's bank was near failure because Hudson had opened a bank in town and had pulled most of the good money into his bank. Brad was left with small depositors and ranchers who had little money, but needed loans each year for their crops and operating capital to carry them through until fall cattle sales.

The small ranchers who held their accounts in Brad's bank always seemed to have bad luck. The sheriff was a fair man, but he had not been able to prove any wrongdoing in the whole string of problems in the valley. Brad was sure that someone was behind the problems that had started just at the time that Clint had left town after his run-in with the law. If these ranch failures didn't stop, Brad would lose his bank. Brad, along with a dozen old-time ranchers and a few of the old small community store owners would all go under together. Brad needed ten thousand dollars now to cover notes that Hudson had gotten his hands on and that had come due. If the ranchers could get one cattle drive through, they could make it. Brad was asking Clint to protect the Crossbow cattle drive. Maybe he could do it without being identified by the law.

Chapter 4.

Even though Clint was the younger brother, when it came to physical harm, violence, or gun play, Brad had always had the utmost trust in Clint. Brad was a businessman, family man and community civic person almost from birth. Even as a child he was liked by the community fathers for his dependability and business savvy. Clint chuckled to himself as he recalled this because his reputation had been almost the opposite— quick to fight, aggressive, disliked business work, rode wild horses through the town streets at top speed. In general, Clint was a regular hell-raiser, as well as the best poker player in town at sixteen and probably the best pistol and rifle shot in the community. At fourteen, Clint recalled winning both the rifle and pistol contest at the annual picnic and county fair. Two years later, when Clint was sixteen, he had so outdone everyone with the pistol and rifle shooting that the picnic organizers changed the rules so that anyone who had won two years in a row could no longer compete. Those men so disqualified were classified as professional gun shooters and could serve only as judges and other support positions. Clint knew right then that the civic leaders had feared him even as a boy, almost a man, but more than that they resented his slightly arrogant style and self-confidence.

Clint also remembered now where he had first heard the name of Captain Carl Hudson, ex-army officer turned gentleman rancher and businessman. He liked to be called Captain, as he regularly introduced himself. Mr. Hudson had been a competing shooter in the contest Clint had won and had been visibly upset when a sixteen-year-old boy had out-shot him in front of all the local citizens. Clint also remembered that it was only six months later that he was driven from Crossbow to never return.

Now here he sat, only a few miles from the county line, trying to decide how to proceed to help his brother, if Brad still needed his help. Matter of fact, Clint didn't even know if his brother was still alive.

Even with all this urgency of mission and the driving desire to see his brother, or at least know what had happened, or was happening to him, Clint never lost his cool calculating mind. He knew his best chance to help his brother was still to follow the original instructions and work behind the scenes. Brad had not wanted Clint to get into trouble by being recognized, even though he no doubt needed his help desperately. That was like his older brother to think of his safety, even when he was the last person he could turn to for help. Brad would never have asked unless he thought that Clint could do the job without too great a risk. Brad had always placed complete confidence in Clint when it came to solving problems with tough people.

Clint's first task was to find out what was going on in Crossbow without being seen. If anyone was rustling cattle in the county they would have to move them either north or south.   The east and west boundaries were made up of steep valley walls that were almost impossible for cattle to climb.   Clint decided to invest a couple of days at each of the two trail towns on either side of Manatee County, Morristown and Clifton. His cave hideout would serve as home base.

Chapter 5.

The next morning's sunrise found Clint and the roan stallion two hours down the trail. The cold rain had put a damp chill in the air, but the night's rest and plenty of cold rainwater to drink had put both man and horse in top shape. Already Clint had decided to spend the week it would take to hang around Morristown, and then to ride back around Manatee County to Clifton so that he could learn what was going into and out of Crossbow. It would also give him a chance to stock up his newly found cave home, or rather rediscovered hideout. It turned out that the cave had been found by Clint's subconscious or memory just below the conscious level. He had found that special hiding place years ago, when, as a young boy, he rode every nook and cranny of this country around Crossbow. Only one other person had ever shared the fun and excitement of that young boy exploring that hideaway.

Morristown was a typical western trading post, bar and stopover town for the wild and reckless life that existed in this rugged territory. Poker playing was the primary past time when the men were not putting in twelve to sixteen hour days on the nearby ranches. Mixed with this rowdy group were peddlers, merchants, drifters, fortune hunters, miners, and drunks. Morristown had two hotel-bar-restaurant combinations and one run-down saloon. The saloon seemed to specialize in poor ranchers and miners who only wanted to drink their booze in peace and pass the time playing penny ante poker.

It was a group of cowboys inside the saloon that Clint selected to lose some money to. The card skills of Clint allowed him to feed enough money into the pot to keep the spirits flowing and raise the sociable level at the table. However, he played it close enough to let them know that he was no tin horn, but only that he allowed the cards to run against him to their benefit. By the second day, Clint had skillfully identified the players by group, such as loyalties, politics, employer and personality. Then, by careful betting and body language, he had bluffed and extracted the money from the less desirable and distributed it to the desirable. This had gradually developed a table of very congenial players who were having a great time playing poker, not losing too much money and talking openly about their jobs, politics, and rumors. By the morning of the third day Clint had learned about all he could from Morristown. He had also moved over to one of the larger hotel bars where the traders, merchants, travel guests and ranch owners spent their gambling monies. Clint had been able to recover all his donations to the poorer class plus a little extra for good measure. By moving around and keeping only a small amount on the table, no one noticed his winnings or his skill. He played the part of a nondescript cowboy in town for a few drinks and some friendly poker.

Clint had purchased enough supplies for several weeks, including extra shells, blankets, and camp gear. He had found an excellent buy on another horse from one of the down and out card-playing cowboys. The horse didn't look like much, but at first glance Clint knew it had power, speed and real heart. The cowboy wanted another horse for show and no doubt never suspected that he had owned probably the best horse in town, if you didn't count Clint's roan. Clint had arranged a three-way trade with the stockman at the local livery stable. The stockman got the money he wanted for a fine looking horse, the cowboy got the best looking horse of all his friends and Clint got the best breeding mare in that town. It's not often that you can do business, with each person leaving with what they think is the best deal. Clint knew how to read people and horse trading was his natural born skill. He could judge a horse as well as he could a man.

Clint was riding the sorrel mare and allowing the roan stallion to run free and feed along the way to camp. After stowing the supplies in the hideaway and placing one of the water barrows so the roan could get to it, Clint rode off on the mare to Clifton, leaving the roan to rest and enjoy life a little. The early spring was bringing fresh grass growth in the valley just below the cave and a few days of grazing and rest should bring the roan back to top condition after the hard six weeks of travel to Crossbow.

Clint had recognized two of the cowboys in Morristown as men he had known back ten to fifteen years ago in Crossbow, but he knew they had no idea of his identity. Clint had changed a lot since his

16

sixteenth birthday. His hair had changed from a blonde towhead to dark brown and the beard stubble was an extra mask. His six-foot-two-inch height was a good five inches more than he was when he had last seen the people of this region. The two hundred and ten pounds of hard muscle, deep chest, and strong hands was in stark contrast to the wiry, slim and fast-paced boy of before. The slow, deliberate walk of Clint was a studied deceptive cover for the cat-quick speed that had carried forward from the boy to the man.

Chapter 6.

Four days had passed since Clint had first looked down on the Crossbow valley. As he entered Clifton from the north, which was the opposite direction from Morristown, Clint had heard a lot about what had happened in Crossbow the last ten years. To his great relief his brother was alive, even if almost financially ruined. The poker players in Morristown had described Brad Mason as a guy who had stood tough against all the bad luck that could befall an individual in business. Almost every loan Brad would grant one of the small businessmen or a much deserving rancher would be followed by some business or ranching failure. Brad had held out for five years against all odds to keep himself and his bank customers afloat. Brad had even borrowed heavily against the old family ranch to provide money to his friends. In the end, Brad had been forced to close his bank and was now running a dry goods store in Crossbow so he could feed his family, hang onto the ranch and pay off his debts. He had won the hearts of Crossbow's long-time citizens through his trust, honesty and support to all who came to him for help over the years. But little could be done by his friends now to repay his kindness, for it seemed the gods had turned against the long-term residents of Manatee Country, particularly the business friends of

18

Brad Mason. It was also rumored that Brad received threats to his family if he didn't get out of the banking business. Although none of the poker players had ever heard any of this from Mr. Mason over all the years they had known him, the rumor still floated around.

With all of this information gathered firmly in Clint's mind, Clifton's saloons were plowed for rumor and seemingly unrelated pieces of information. Clifton was occupied by a different type of western manpower. Clint identified at least a dozen professional gunmen killing time at the card tables. The average cowhand was in short supply and stayed out of the three big Main Street saloons.

Clint quickly found the hangout of the working cowboys. It was a side street saloon where they could spend their hard earned dollars and have it last long enough to be worth working another month to do it all again. Clint applied the same card playing techniques and quickly weeded out the rough necks by cleaning out their money and built-up the easy talking, friendly type stack of chips. It appeared that as soon as the card playing group felt sure that they were among friends, and that the almost silent Clint was a non-threatening body, the rumors and facts flowed like water. It was as if most of these guys knew something was wrong, but had been afraid to exchange rumors with each other, each not being sure of who was safe to talk to. Clint's magical ability to select the right birds of a similar feather provided this small group of six players to have one of the most enjoyable two days in Clifton that they could ever remember. It was also a miracle that Sunday afternoon, as each headed out to their respective ranch jobs for another month, they still had money in their pockets. Clint had been able to transfer almost two hundred dollars of his previous winnings into those good old boys' hands without their suspecting a thing. The information that Clint had received was worth far more than a few hundred dollars. Besides, Clint intended to replenish his operating monies at the three plush saloons on Main Street.

One thing was real apparent. Someone was slowly and carefully bleeding the old-time ranchers to death. It was being done with such skill that even the most astute ranch owners were not picking up on the scheme. It all dated back to about the time Clint had left Crossbow. The grazing land in Manatee County was some of the finest in New Mexico. A few thousand acres in this valley could produce more pounds of beef than ten thousand acres of other land in this whole territory. That was one reason that Clint's and Brad's dad had stopped his western move when he laid eyes on this protected valley, fertile soil and ample water supply.

Old man Mason and five other settlers carved out ranches by mutual agreement, each bordering the main river bed for water during extreme dry spells and extending their property lines to the protective rim that ran down the east and west borders of Manatee County. The higher elevations gave good grass during the hot summer months, whereas the protected valley provided ideal grazing throughout the winter. Butch Mason, as most old-timers had known their dad, rather than the Alexander Lee Mason handle that their grandmother had hooked onto their dad at his birth, had planned well and was trusted by the other five original ranchers. That was one reason why the Mason ranch set at the north head of the valley and straddled the headwaters of Manatee County.

Water is the gold of western property and the lifeblood of any ranching community. The other ranchers knew that as long as Butch Mason controlled the source of Manatee's surface water they would each have access to their fair share.

Clint was entering the third Main Street saloon to extract the last few hundred dollars from the loud and noisy gunslingers, miners and some very arrogant business types when he spotted two men that, to Clint's experienced eyes, were true professional killers. The smooth style, expensive tools of the trade and cautious manners gave away only a hint of the trouble packaged within these men. The eyes of each told Clint more than he wanted to know. As the tension within Clint tightened, his outward appearance became more and more relaxed and casual. A poker seat in just the right location came available and Clint eased into it as wearily as a trail hand just off six weeks of pushing a thousand dumb cows over rough terrain. Clint made a mental note to avoid any attention to himself or else these experienced gunmen might make a similar assessment of him. These two were the type Clint had been looking for. A scheme that was planned and executed over many years could only rely on top firepower. Whoever had invested the time and money to capture a whole county by subtle, behind the scenes operations would occasionally need physical force.

Also, if subtle means ever hit a snag, then the real firepower could be brought to bear on the obstruction. After a few hours of observation, Clint confirmed his initial opinion. These gents were here to stay. They had plenty of money and no one got in their way. Clint pulled a little less than he had intended from the easy pickings and lost the last few hands so no one thought anything when he excused himself and slowly disappeared into the crowd and out the door.

Clint now knew who to focus his attention on to start unraveling this elaborate operation that had bankrupted his brother and most of the other original ranchers. These two skilled gun toters were not the mastermind, but you could bet ten to one that they were the leaders of a core of a rough and tumble group of fighters that could be brought to action with just a signal. Getting a fix on the strength of that group was a must. Know your enemy and never underestimate his strength or intelligence.

The other piece of information that was most interesting was the out movement of hundreds of cattle every few months through this northern passage. No one had said so, but just enough tidbits of information were collected by Clint to make that conclusion with a high degree of assurance. This would narrow the area that Clint would have to cover. He must find out where the cattle were being taken and who was managing the whole operation.

A more urgent problem was the loss of the old family ranch. Clint had picked up a rumor that Brad Mason was being forced to transfer title of the ranch to Captain Carl Hudson. The ever-popular Hudson had let it be known that he had acquired the loan papers on the Mason ranch and to assure that the title to this valuable piece of property did not get into outsiders' hands, he was forced to take title. He would allow Brad to keep any of his personal possessions and a few head of cattle and horses for his family's use on their only remaining property, the little ten acre ranchette near Crossbow city limits. Brad had lived there the past few years so he could spend more time making what little money he could with long hours at the dry goods store. Although Brad had never considered himself much of a rancher, he had done a successful job after his father's death and up until shortly after Clint was driven out of town. Then the ranch seemed to have one disaster after another. The barn burned full of hay. Over one hundred head of his choice stock had disappeared the first year.

The loss of the cattle hurt Clint as much as, if not more than, losing the barn. Clint, at fifteen, had taken a couple hundred dollars of his and Brad's hard earned money and had gone over to Santa Fe. After long bargaining he had obtained and single-handedly driven thirty head of the best beef stock in the country back to their ranch as the core of their breeding herd. The quality of their herd was already showing up when Clint left Crossbow.

As the scattered pieces of information were diligently and carefully gathered by Clint, each fact was seared into his mind as a lasting impression, as if branded there by a hot iron. As the desperate plight of Brad was unfolded, the pain and humiliation that Brad must have felt was relived by Clint. The pieces of bad information burned his inner soul, almost like a branding iron to tender yearling hide.

Clint had to find a way to keep the Mason ranch from being lost. If rumors were close to right, Brad had to put up the ranch as collateral with a Santa Fe bank to cover the loans of his neighbor ranchers. When the ranchers continued to have bad luck, outside investors called in the loans on the valley ranches, including the Mason ranch. Brad had worked financial miracles over the past ten years holding off the creditors, each year giving the valley one more chance to meet its loan payments. Most of the friendly cowboys spoke with a hint of pride and admiration when they talked about how Brad Mason, the small town banker and rancher, had stood tough against long odds. They all accepted the impending defeat as inevitable. And even in defeat and financial failure, the select few poker players, both in Clifton and Morristown, continued to secretly hope that this honest and caring community supporter could be saved.

Clint found the telegraph office and sent off a brief message to the Santa Fe bank, asking what amount of cash payment would delay for six months the foreclosure on Brad Mason's ranch in Manatee County, New Mexico. The reply was to be sent to Brad Mason's new stockbreeder under the initials C.M. at the Clifton, New Mexico telegraph office. The next day Clint had his answer; three thousand dollars was needed within one week to hold off the foreclosure for six months.

Clint's poker skills were almost phenomenal, but even with that, how much money could he extract from a small western town without being identified and his cover blown? Clint had more than enough back in the hideaway, but could he get there, return and send the money by stage to Santa Fe before the week was up? He checked his total cash on hand with winnings from both Morristown and Clifton monies, excluding the monies he had carefully fed back to the friendly cowboys. He now wished he had not been so generous. Even so, he had just shy of two thousand dollars. That meant he must get another one thousand dollars by no later than the Wednesday morning stage. That left him Monday and Tuesday night. Most of the working cowboys had left town Sunday, so most of the remaining men were fair game for fleecing, but carefully. The game plan for getting control of the valley depended on his identity not being learned.

The major source of gambling funds in this town was in the Copper Nickel, which was the same saloon where the two professional gunslingers hung out. Clint did not want to underestimate the talent of those two.

Wednesday morning found Clint weary, but relieved that he had just made the stage with his package and a telegram to the bank giving the details of the monies that would arrive by stage.

Chapter 7.

The poker playing had been successful in getting the cash from the cattle buyers, mine operators and some very cash-rich, heavily armed supposed cowboys. One of the top guns had joined the card playing late Tuesday night and had stayed close to Clint until he lost him through some quick thinking on toilet needs, feeding his face twice and tending his horse. Clint didn't think the gun hand called Ron was aware of how much money Clint had won or that he had sneaked it out on the stage, but Ron's curiosity was definitely raised to a high level, which only meant trouble for Clint. Now that the bank had been put off for six months, the next step of the plan must be started. To stop the accidents in a whole county single handedly and not be identified was not going to be an easy task. Both of the two gunmen, Ron and his sidekick Tom, had plenty of money to spend. This reinforced Clint's assessment that they were good, real good.

Clint did not take himself too seriously as to his ability with the well-worn Colt 44 at his side. He never took anything for granted when his life depended on it. A week did not pass that both pistol and rifle practice wasn't taken. It was not a chore because the power and smooth motion of his cared-for shooting equipment was always a source of satisfaction and a feeling of accomplishment. It was similar to an artist who keeps trying portraits. Once he can reproduce the living likeness of an individual through his drawings, he strives to keep that skill and improve on it, because of the satisfaction that he feels inside. If Clint had been asked to explain why a thing of such potential violence and sometimes death could also give such pride, he would have been lost for words. Clint had never used his shooting skills against people unless forced against the wall. Over the past several years he had been forced against the wall many times and his unscratched body attested to his level of skill. Even Clint's boyhood shooting accomplishments were discounted by him with the excuse that all that shooting had been at targets. The true life test was facing the risk of death and still being able to go through the same lightning smooth draw and firing that was done in the secrecy of remote practices.

The Santa Fe bank responded with a very nice telegram to acknowledge the payment. Additional comments indicated that they were very willing to cooperate. Apparently, Brad's good reputation was even known in the Santa Fe banking area. No doubt he had done a lot of business with them besides just the ranch loan. With this problem resolved for the present, Clint decided to set up a surveillance of cattle and people movement through the northern pass out of Manatee County. Clint returned to his cave hideaway several times over the next two weeks to trade horses and rest in relative security with both horses acting as sentinels. The mare had adopted her new master with complete loyalty and was a companion to the stallion from the first day. Clint allowed the mare to roam free when he was out with the stallion, even when he would be gone for several days. A corralled or staked-out horse would be a dead giveaway. Clint was being extremely careful to protect himself and his identity. When the people behind this scheme learned of the payment to the Santa Fe bank on Brad's loan all hell could break loose. Clint knew too much time and manpower had been put into this undercover operation for them to lose the valley ranches when the last few ranches were on the brink of falling into their hands.

Clint was sure that Captain Hudson was the focal point even though he was still very well thought of in the valley community. His arrival into the community had just preceded the occurrence of unexplained accidents in Manatee County, though. Clint had also learned that Ron Johnson, apparently "gunslinger number one," had arrived in the area about two years behind Captain Hudson.

Ron's presence in Manatee County also matched the period of time when cattle loss started and several shootings took the lives of some key ranch hands and owners. Two of the most public killings occurred in Clifton over card cheating. Tom Townsend was the gambler who, on two separate occasions, had accused one of the key ranch owners of cheating at cards. Both ranchers were goaded into defending themselves and their honor and had lost to the swift gun toter, Tom. Since that time most of the ranchers and regular cowhands had avoided playing cards at the same table with Tom. Tom or Ron did not seem to have any means of support, but they ate, drank and dressed well. They stayed in the best hotel in town and rode the best looking horses at the hitching rails. Both men frequently left town for several days at a time. Clint had also put together their past absences of longer periods of time to match those when fairly large losses of cattle had occurred in Manatee County.

The start of Clint's third week of watching the trails north of Clifton finally paid off. Over two hundred head of prime stock were being moved north through an obscure trail that by-passed Clifton. Clint had spotted the trail the first week and had kept fairly close watch over it. Five heavily armed men were working the cattle north in no hurry. It seemed they did not worry about lookouts and had used this trail before.

Clint had identified the best place along the trail to take charge. He felt five to one was about right; he didn't want to take too much advantage of these rustlers. Clint had identified the brands. They were all from the target ranches, including the Mason ranch. He also noted that a lot of the cattle were not branded. Clint was just about to place a well-aimed rifle shot through the shooting arm of the nearest rider when a flash of reflected sunshine caught his eye. Slowly moving through the cover just below the ridge top, but above Clint's position, was Tom Townsend with rifle drawn and ready for action. Now Clint understood why the other five rustlers were not watching their trail very close. Clint knew if he could get Tom out of the way, the others might not want to pursue the fight.

Tom no doubt had done this guard duty many times before and had gotten a little over confident. Clint worked his way up to within fifty feet of Tom before Clint saw Tom's back straighten and go cold still. Clint didn't expect Tom's next move, Tom dove out of his saddle with his pistol firing as he hit the ground. Pure luck kept Clint alive. Quick reaction and deadly aim left Tom dead with a single bullet through his head and down through his body.

Tom had gotten off three shots as he rolled. One had gone wild, but the first two had gone into the tree trunk, not six inches to the right of Clint. It was Clint's shot that had caught Tom just before his third shot and no doubt saved the day for Clint. Clint had never seen such shooting before. No ordinary gun hand could have gotten those two shots off before Clint fired his controlled, deadly round.

Clint had left his horse back a ways before sneaking up on Tom's back trail. He was on foot, which could prove rather bad for Clint if the other five horsemen decided to stand and fight. The five had left the herding job and had fanned out in a half circle around the place where the shooting noise had come from. Clint moved about fifty yards off to one side and dropped the closest rustler with a deep shot into his shooting shoulder. Clint quickly moved back to the place where Tom lay dead and fired another rifle shot into the man the longest distance away. Clint was thankful he had carried his rifle with him when trailing Tom. Carrying a rifle in one hand and his pistol in the other had slowed him with Tom, but a handgun alone would be no match against five riders with rifles. The second man had gone down with a bullet through his thigh. It had also hit the man's horse, which Clint regretted. With two men down and no response from Tom when they called his name, the remaining men's will to continue this battle was disappearing. Clint moved to his left this time and placed a good shot into the last fleeing rider.

Clint quickly searched the two downed, unconscious men for identification, money and weapons. Between Tom's body and the two wounded rustlers, Clint obtained just under one thousand dollars. Tom alone had been carrying almost eight hundred dollars in cash and gold coins. Tom's rifle was one of the latest level action models. Most gun owners would almost kill to get their hands on such a rifle. After finding a nearby hiding place for the loot, Clint raced back into Clifton and got into a card game as casually as possible. He had tried to be regular enough in pattern to establish an alibi and keep suspicion away from himself.

Chapter 8.

Clint had taken just long enough to search everyone, hide the loot and hide Tom's body. Tom's horse had been unsaddled and turned loose about midway back to town. Even with all that loss of time, Clint was well into the poker games before one of the rustlers came into the saloon and pulled Ron aside. Ron's eyes almost immediately turned to Clint, as the rustler no doubt related the shootout and the time Clint had entered the saloon. Clint, with absolute control, played a lazy hand of poker under the watchful eyes of Ron. Ron sent the other gunman outside. After fifteen to twenty minutes the gunman returned and Clint could see him shaking his head "no" as he reported to Ron. Clint had hidden his horse before entering the saloon. A hot, sweating horse could have caused Clint some real problems as he tried to appear as if he had always been loafing around town and playing poker. Clint was sure that none of the five rustlers had seen him well enough to identify him. The way Clint had moved around, he was sure that Ron was being told that several men had jumped them. They were also relaying that they had gone back to get the two downed riders and had looked for Tom, but never found him after the shooting was over.

The rumors soon spread throughout Clifton that some group of men had shot up Ron's gun handling wranglers. Word was also gotten to some of the Manatee County ranchers that over two hundred head of their stock had been seen roaming with no one tending them on the trail northwest of Clifton. Clint knew he must stop these raids on valley ranchers. He would not help his brother if he got himself killed. The shootout with Tom had been much too close and if Clint's assessment was right about Ron, he was even more dangerous than Tom.

Ron joined the poker game where Clint was playing, but very soon the other players excused themselves one by one until only Clint and Ron were left. A tense stillness settled over the saloon. Everyone knew that Ron's men had been shot up and he was on the prod. The unlucky man that ended up being the last one at the table with Ron stood a good chance of playing his last card game on this earth. For a few minutes Ron just sat there looking Clint over as Clint slowly shuffled the cards. The room was so quiet that only the sound of the cards could be heard. But from Clint's outward appearance, you would have thought he was sitting on a peaceful riverbank somewhere just waiting for the fish to bite. Clint's casual remark, "Ron, are you in or out, you're a nickel short," was like a crack of thunder in the room. People were looking for a place to hide if shooting broke out. You could read in the bar crowd faces that this drifting cowboy was about to meet his maker and probably knew nothing about the risk he was facing as he waited for Ron to either ante up or end the card game.

Without a comment Ron got up from the table and left the saloon. Immediately, several of the card players came over and informed Clint that he could have been killed. They knew he was fairly new to town and surely didn't know that Ron was the fastest gun hand in these parts. They told him how lucky he was to be alive and that he should maybe leave town for a few days. One cowboy named Dan said he had talked to his ramrod on Circle J about hiring another man for a few months until they could make a small cattle drive. Circle J had lost about fifty head of cattle to rustlers only two weeks earlier and if they didn't sell some stock soon the ranch would be lost. The ranch could not pay Clint anything but room and board until they sold some cattle. Dan had played cards with Clint and knew he was the soft-spoken type that would feel at home at the Circle J. Dan also told Clint that the Mason ranch next door was being foreclosed and the owner, Brad Mason, had moved to town to work at his dry goods store.

Clint accepted the offer. This job would put him close to the home ranch and maybe allow him to better prevent the loss of any more cattle out of the county. Between the Mason and the Circle J ranches, the northern part of Manatee County pass was now covered.

Dan Sexton accepted the name of Cliff Martin without a question, as is usual in these western areas. Any name will do; people are much more interested in what you are now than what you were in the past. A man is measured by his performance and skill rather than words. It also goes that they don't trust you until you have proven yourself. The Circle J was now owned by Alice Jordan. She was a smart looking lady in her early twenties, slender built, but ranch tough. Her dad and older brother had both been killed three years ago when a herd they were driving north to Santa Fe had been stampeded. Alice had borrowed money from Captain Hudson the last two years just to keep the ranch going and pay the hands enough to keep them in food and clothing.

The ranch was getting the run down look because only enough men were kept on to tend the shrinking herd. The fences and barns were in need of a lot of repair. Money was needed for repair supplies, lumber, wire and even roofing. However, the grazing land was in top shape. The loss of cattle had given the ranges a chance to overgrow. Clint also noticed that there were very few young calves and yearlings. This was really curious since the cows looked in excellent condition.

Alice Jordan was not very friendly when Dan introduced Clint as Cliff Martin. Ben Toss was the ramrod/foreman and seemed to be the low key, nonviolent type that just wanted to ranch. He explained that Alice was usually a very good-natured person, but the stress of the last few years was taking its toll. Ben also filled in that Alice had not wanted to spend any more money on new hands because all cash was coming from loans through Captain Hudson. Hudson was trying to get Alice to join him, hopefully through marriage, and put her ranch with his, which lay just south. Ben relayed this to the new hand, not as gossip, but as facts that might affect his decision to work on the Circle J. Hudson had promised that the old regular hands of the Circle J would be kept on, but any part-time and seasonal workers would not have jobs after this season. Clint said that did not bother him since he was only drifting through.

Clint, over the next month, with summer well under way, kept busy doing the ranch work of three men during the day and by night secretly patrolling the northern edge of the Circle J and the Big M, as the Mason ranch was known. The breakup of the two hundred head drive by Tom's group really excited the valley ranchers. The cattle were rounded up and returned to the respective owners. The Circle J's fifty head loss of several weeks earlier was in the recovered cattle. The Big M got back forty and the other ranchers got five to ten each as the brands were identified. The unbranded were evenly divided among the ranches.

Chapter 9.

It was rumored that Tom had been out-gunned and rather than return and face the music from Ron, had skipped town. Clint kept this idea alive by finding Tom's horse and moving it to a remote grazing spot in the northeast corner of the Mason ranch so it would not be found. Brad still had a small band of horses in that area that were used only if they were making a big cattle drive. Tom's splendid looking horse did sort of stand out in this cast-off lot of working ranch horses. Clint thought that if Tom's stallion would breed some of these working mares, the Big M ranch could really improve their riding stock. Tom would probably turn over in his hidden grave if he knew his efforts to ruin the Big M had turned out to have a long term benefit.

Clint had agreed to work out of the north range summer cabin. Clint made the point to Ben Toss, the ramrod, that he could cover that area by himself where usually three men worked all summer. Ben had seen Clint's work those first few weeks and didn't need any extra persuasion. The ranch was real shorthanded and two extra hands around the ranch headquarters and the south end would make life a lot better for the foreman and the other hands. The few times Ben visited the north range he could not believe the work Clint had done on his own. The water holes were clean, the herds were moved around together. Clint had killed a dozen coyotes and one mountain lion that had been a regular menace to the herds. The cabin roof and water well had been repaired and a huge supply of firewood had been stacked nearby. Ben would leave a note and food supplies each visit because he never saw Clint and assumed he was off working another section.

Clint had gotten into the ranch work with a real feeling of satisfaction. The hard work was like a tonic to both his body and his mind. He was working twelve to sixteen hours each day, then sleeping along the trails three or four nights per week. He had spotted an occasional rider, but no movement of cattle since the shootout with Tom's group. But Clint knew that whoever was behind this was only regrouping for another approach to take over the valley.

Clint had slipped away to his hideaway after the first week and brought both his horses to the north range cabin. It was during that trip that Clint finally realized what was going on with the age of the valley cattle. He had found at least a dozen bulls and male calves dead and partially hidden. Someone was bleeding the valley to death, but saving the breeding cows so that when the foreclosures came, they could bring in some breeding bulls and produce an excellent yearly crop of calves the first year. This method had cut off the ranchers' supply of annual income, but did not take away the ranches' inherent value. The rustling was enough to keep everyone looking at this problem while providing cash to the people behind the scheme.

Time was running out for the Circle J. Apparently, word had gotten back to Captain Hudson about the delay in taking over the Big M ranch, so extra pressure was being put on Alice Jordan, owner of the Circle J. The word was out that Alice and Captain Carl Hudson were planning to be married by fall. There was almost twenty years between them, but Captain Hudson was a striking figure in appearance, with apparently plenty of money and power.

Being midsummer now, Clint had gone down to the main house to suggest that Ben Toss consider moving more cattle to the northern range. Clint's managing of the herd up there by moving them around in a large group had allowed the herd to cut down the grass fairly short in a small area, but not trample the whole range. When the cattle were moved to another area, the short grass would quickly grow. Clint had seen this type of range management done in some very dry ranches in Arizona. It proved to be just as effective in this good grazing land. Keeping the cattle close to water, in a small area and keeping away any predators had allowed the stock to put on some good weight. Clint had also found an excellent breeding bull in one of the isolated northern pastures. In a contained area, this one bull could service almost three or four times as many cows spread out over the whole range. Clint knew by early next spring the Circle J would have a big crop of new calves. Clint had also moved as many stray Big M cows into the Circle J herd as he could find. Big M had given up on ranching their northern area. That was due, no doubt, to the past history of losing almost anything that was run up there.

Clint figured that come spring, both Circle J and Big M ranches would have a new generation of top quality beef in the spring calf dropping. The bull that Clint had found was one of the best beef bulls that Clint had seen. In fact, it looked a lot like the breed line that Clint himself had gotten up near Santa Fe over ten years ago.

Most of the cattle found over these last two months were without brands, so Clint had taken to branding the cattle as he found them. If on Circle J land then they got a Circle J brand, if on Big M, then he used his Big M brand. Now Clint knew why it had been easy for the rustlers to remove all the young stock from the northern ranges over the last few years. Once the ranchers gave up on trying to manage the northern region, the rustlers, apparently, each year removed any unbranded stock plus any additional bulls they found. The rustlers probably only moved out branded stock when they either needed more or felt they needed to keep the pressure on the ranchers.

Ben Toss was glad to hear that the northern range could take more cattle, but he told Clint that each year they had lost most of the stock they had moved up there and what they didn't lose, did not drop calves the following spring. Ben felt that with the smaller herd that the ranch now had on the lower southern and central grazing areas, the grass would hold out. The summer temperature would keep the cattle from gaining as much weight as the cooler northern pastures, but the risk was too great. Ben lavished praise on Clint in front of the other cowboys, but everyone seemed to agree. Clint didn't know if they really were impressed with the work he was doing up there alone or if they just really appreciated being allowed to stay at the ranch bunkhouse all summer. It is a lot better living around the headquarters than out in those range cabins. Besides, Alice Jordan personally oversaw the menu and stayed after the cook to provide good meals to the ranch hands. Alice seemed to have the attitude that if they were going to lose the ranch, at least her men, many of whom had been with her father before, would enjoy good eating and housing up to the very last. Alice and the men knew that when Captain Hudson combined the two ranches following the marriage the old lifestyle would be gone. No one talked about it, but most of the old timers were planning to move on come next summer. They would stay through the coming winter and help with spring roundup then head out, even if they didn't know where they were going.

Clint spent only one day and one night at the headquarters before taking supplies and heading back to his northern post. He didn't want to be gone very long, because he knew by a feeling in his bones that trouble was pending. No one seemed to question Clint's urgency to return to his remote outpost. Many cowboys were loners and Clint's quiet manner put him in that category. Clint thanked Ben and Alice for giving him a job that took him out of Clifton and the threat of Ron. They all accepted this as if proud of their good deed in saving his life. No ordinary cowboy had a chance against Ron Johnson. Clint learned that two more cowboys had been shot in Clifton by Ron. One was killed and the other would probably never be able to ride herd again. Both men were prodded into drawing over a barroom brawl. The sheriff had ruled both fights fair.

Chapter 10.

Clint was scouting the northern ranch boundary the next morning when off to his right he could hear mounted riders. He dropped off his horse and led him to some thick pine and scrub oak cover. Within minutes a dozen men passed through the wooded area not thirty yards from Clint's hiding spot. With a firm but gentle hand over the big roan's nose the two of them stood in silence as the band under Ron's leadership moved on south. They were all heavily armed but outfitted to work cattle. Clint knew a new try was going to be made on the valley herds.

The dozen men had outriders and were very alert. Luck had again been with Clint that he had heard them first, but years of living on the edge of danger had conditioned Clint to be alert at all times. His mind would monitor the environment without his conscious effort, but when something unusual was noted, his conscious mind was brought into action. When the band of gun toting rustlers had moved south downrange about a mile, Clint could feel his muscles relax and he noticed his more rapid breathing. A brief smile crossed his face as he noted the body responses that he had long learned to live with and that more than once had saved his hide. This group was well seasoned and nobody's fools, so Clint would have to use utmost caution if he was to track them and not be detected. The surprise attack on Tom's group was no doubt still well remembered.

The dilemma facing Clint was one of too many riders for him to handle by himself with no way to warn the ranch, because the band was between him and the ranch.

The band of gunmen continued to keep under cover of the timber but headed in a fairly straight line for the Circle J's largest grazing herd that Clint knew was being held in the southwest corner of the range. The Circle J crew that now numbered only six was trying to hold together as many yearlings as possible for full market. They were using some of Clint's suggestions and were moving the herd very slowly from watering hole to watering hole over the best grazing pastures in the southern ranch area. With at least two men either at the main ranch complex or out gathering and distributing supplies nearly all the time, that would leave only four cowboys to defend the herd against a dozen well-seasoned gun hands. In addition, the advantage of surprise would be on the crooks' side.

Clint had moved within one half mile of the band when they spread out. At first Clint thought he had pressed his luck too far by getting so close. However, Ron had his men spread along a fighting line just below a long ridge. Clint surmised that the unsuspecting Circle J crew was just over that ridge. Clint slid out of the saddle and putting Tom's expensive rifle on a rest, he sighted in on the middle rider and squeezed the trigger. The man just tumbled out of the saddle. A few seconds later, as the sound reached the band of outlaws, there was confusion for a few seconds. Ron immediately took charge and, probably thinking that one of the Circle J riders had spotted them, lead the charge over the ridge into battle.

Clint knew that he couldn't do any more for the Circle J than the one warning shot he had taken. Hopefully, they would run for it and let Ron's gang take the cattle. But the rapid firing of rifles and pistols soon told Clint that the Circle J crew was either pinned down or had decided to go down fighting.

Clint rode as fast as he could across the opening and the small valley and into the timber on the east side. If Ron and his gang came back this way, maybe he could confuse them. He had just made it into the heavy underbrush when the first few head of cattle started moving over the ridge heading north. Several riders appeared, with Ron directing the drive. Clint only counted eight men, so, with the one he had gotten, the Circle J must have put up a real fight to take out three more. Clint had been right to move from his original firing position for when Ron drew near the place he took two riders and really combed the area. Ron must have had some real training or experience to have followed the line of that one half-mile shot to almost its exact spot. Clint had left that spot headed away from the valley at a rapid run, but once he hit a hard rock outcrop, he had slowed his horse and carefully moved off to one side before heading back across the valley to his present hiding place. This deception seemed to work, for when Ron and the other two followed the tracks up to the rock outcrop, they seemed to be satisfied that the rider had headed out after taking the one pot shot, which had proven deadly even at this range. They also may not have wanted to ride into an ambush with anyone that could shoot that good.

When the rustlers had moved the herd out of site on a due north course, Clint went to see if anything was left of the Circle J crew. Dan Sexton was still alive but bleeding badly. Relief came over Dan as he made out Clint. He couldn't stop telling Clint how the warning shot had given them a chance to give Ron's gang a real run for their money. Dan only wanted Clint to let Alice Jordan know that her men had stood tough against that dozen hired guns. He knew she would be proud of all of them. Clint did what he could to stop the bleeding and with two of the horses, he hooked up a sling with poles and blankets, then headed back to the main ranch with Dan.

Dan never regained consciousness after they got to the ranch. The loss of the four hands and the cattle was the final blow for the Circle J. Alice informed Ben Toss, the foreman, that the struggle was over. She was moving to Crossbow as soon as the funerals were over. Alice told Ben, Clint and Joe, the only help she had outside the cook, that she was sure that Carl Hudson would take them on, for he was a generous man and his ranch had not had the problems that she had experienced the last five years.

With Dan never being able to tell Alice and Ben how Clint had given them a warning shot and taken out one of the rustlers, Clint gave all the credit to the four Circle J hands. He expanded on the rustlers' loss of four out of their twelve. Clint said he was returning to the ranch for some supplies when he heard the shooting in the far distance. By the time he had gotten there, the gang was gone with the herd. Dan had been left for dead but had revived enough to relay the story and identify Ron Johnson as the leader. Clint did not tell Alice or Ben that Dan had also identified one of the men in the gang as Chuck Rogers, a man who worked for Captain Hudson on the Captain H Ranch.

Clint thanked Miss Jordan for all she had done but said he would stay a little longer at the north range cabin until she could send some of the riders over from Captain Hudson's outfit to drive them south. Clint said she should get a pretty good dollar for the northern herd from Captain Hudson because they were all branded and in excellent condition. Clint said he would visit Clifton every few days and see what he could find to do. Alice said she would send his pay to the general store in Clifton as soon as she could. She thanked Clint for the excellent job he had done and Ben agreed with a statement that if Circle J had a couple more hands like Cliff Martin, they could make the Circle J pay off its debts in no time.

As Clint headed back north, he had a very special purpose in mind. He was more convinced than ever that Captain Hudson was behind this whole operation. Clint, by using his single tube spyglass, had gotten a good look at all of Ron's men several times. First, when they rode right by him and then, while he trailed them. He knew that he could identify each of them if they crossed his path again. This was all-out war and

William F. Martin

he didn't intend to give them any chances if the opportunity presented itself.

Chapter 11.

His main goal right now was to prevent the marriage of Carl Hudson and Alice Jordan. She deserved much more than the likes of him. The loss of the Circle J to Hudson left only the Big M ranch between Hudson and the northern pass. Once that was obtained, Hudson could move cattle out of the region without being observed.

A more important problem could be the water rights. If the headwaters were dammed off as they passed through the Big M ranch, the total water supply of Manatee County could be jeopardized during any hot, dry summer.

Clint had not followed the old cattle trails very far north during his earlier scouting. He had lost three days since the raid on Circle J, but Clint had stayed with Alice Jordan and Ben Toss until the four loyal hands had been placed in their final resting place near the main ranch house. Clint followed the cold trail for three more days, well beyond Clifton into the rugged country of Boyd County. Clint had heard it said several times over drinks and cards by more than one cowboy, that Boyd County had become the marketplace for stolen cattle. The eastern buyers were eager for beef and didn't care where it came from or who was the rightful owner, as long as the beef was in good shape and the price right. Quick profit was the password in this rugged abandoned land. Boyd County lay between the rich fertile valley of Manatee County and the railroad stockyards south of Santa Fe. The eastern cattle buyers could stay in the plush Spanish hotels in Santa Fe and live the good life off the hard work of the ranchers. Clint didn't know which group he hated most, the rough and ruthless gunslinger rustlers or the smooth talking, rich living, quick profit cattle buyers. Without the cattle buyers insisting on proof of ownership for any major herd brought in, it was an open invitation for rustlers. The rustlers would take thirty cents on the dollar for the cattle and the cattle buyers could pocket the other seventy cents.

Clint found the place where the herd had been turned over to another set of drovers. One of the horseshoes on this new set of tracks had a fancy star. Clint had seen similar handy work on dude ranch horses that were rented by eastern businessmen while spending time in the west.

Clint was now four days away from the Circle J northern range cabin. He had told Alice, or Miss Jordan, that he would look after the herd until someone came after them. However, no one seemed too interested. All the will to fight and resist had gone out of the Circle J boss.

Clint had decided it was better to go after the rustlers and try to cut them down one by one and destroy the will of the gunslingers. Clint knew they had lost heavily over the past few weeks. First the mysterious shootout of Tom's group and the loss of the two hundred head they were driving north. No one had seen Tom again. Then this simple task of a dozen well-armed gunmen taking a herd away from four regular ranch hands had turned into a costly battle with Ron losing four men. Clint knew how the minds of these guns-for-hire worked and when the odds got anywhere close to even they didn't want any part of it. If he could get two or three more of these crooks, then all this firepower would panic and leave the country.

Time was running out. Hudson may have the key ranches legally tied up before Clint could carry out his plan. Clint's past life style had conditioned him to deal with the world as he found it. If he could find the buyer he would serve as judge, jury, and executioner. The herd was still in the loading pens when Clint arrived at the stockyard. It didn't take long for the identity of the buyer to be mentioned by the wranglers working the stockyards. Most of these cowhands didn't like eastern dudes who rode rented horses, didn't know a thing about the western life style and flaunted their money and buying power over the local ranchers.

Clint learned that a short heavy-set eastern buyer had bought this herd at less than half the going price. The buyer had also forced the few ranchers who had brought their own herds in to take what he was offering or keep their cattle. Most of the ranchers had no choice but to sell. The stockyard workers also laughingly mentioned that the buyer was riding the big white horse with the star-pattern horseshoes. The local dude ranch had put the special horseshoes on, so the story goes, so that when the eastern gents rented that horse and got themselves lost, at least the dude ranch could track and recover their horse and maybe the rider, if he was still alive. Clint also heard that the eastern buyer who called himself Jeff Lackston played a lot of cards.

Chapter 12.

Clint roved around Santa Fe all afternoon until he located the buyers' hangout. Mr. Lackston had settled into an after-dinner card game at the far end of the saloon. The saloon manager was trying to get a few more players to join the table so the eastern buyer could have a good time playing cards. Clint heard several of the cowboys decline with some comments of how Mr. Lackston usually bought the pot by bluffing out the low financed cowhands.

Clint spread a few extra dollars on the counter to look for change to pay for his drink. Clint knew that the bartender would signal the saloon manager that a new fresh blood was here to be fleeced.

When Clint was asked to join the table he put up just enough resistance, but not enough to be passed over. Clint asked about table stakes and limits and was satisfied inwardly that he couldn't be bluffed out of a pot with the big money of the buyer or the other two major players in the game. There were from outward appearances three well-dressed men with plenty of money and three ordinary cowhands with a little hard earned money who enjoyed the risk of gambling.

Clint soon found that Mr. Lackston was not a very good player, but one of the other well-dressed gents was very skilled in the art of poker. This set the perfect stage for Clint. He could play off the buyer against the smooth professional player and extract a fairly large bundle before they got smart. Then Clint would be in a position to take the dude for all he was worth, if he could string him along with enough hope of recovering his losses.

It was about midnight when the other two cowboys dismissed themselves, realizing they were out of their league. Clint had accumulated several thousand dollars in cash, but had kept the stack in front of himself moderate in size. He had taken the opportunity to cash in a lot of chips on two different occasions when a rest break had been called by the cattle buyer.

The cattle buyer was beginning to realize that he was losing a lot of money and was focusing his comments on the gambler. Clint knew the gambler was already getting wise to who was winning at this table. About two a.m., Mr. Lackston asked that the card game be recessed until ten a.m. after a morning rest and some breakfast. All agreed and the party broke up very peacefully. Clint was sure the last two hands that he let Mr. Lackston win were enough to hook his greed and he would return with a lot more money to take up where he had left off.

Clint sought out the Santa Fe banker the next morning before the card game was to start. A brief explanation was given to the banker of who Clint was and what had happened. The Circle J ranch was going under due to the killing of the four ranch hands and the loss of their main herd.

Clint identified himself as Cliff Martin, the "C.M." messenger who had sent the money for Brad Mason and was here to transfer some more cash to hold off the Mason ranch foreclosure. The banker was delighted because he had worked a lot with Brad Mason over the past ten years and didn't know a more honest businessman and rancher. He explained that he had extended Brad's credit as far as possible and was being pressured by Captain Carl Hudson to foreclose. The cash that had arrived earlier was all the banker needed to do what he always wanted to do, give Brad another chance.

The banker said all that was left of Brad's debt on the ranch was eight thousand dollars, which was not much for a ranch the size of Big M. However, since the ranch had not made a profit in over five years, the bank had been forced by Hudson to start foreclosure.

Mr. Jenson, the banker, was very excited when Clint produced three thousand dollars cash to go against the Big M loan. Mr. Jenson said that he would personally come up with the other five thousand dollars and close out Hudson's lien on the Mason ranch. Clint got Mr. Jenson to promise not to reveal the source of the funds. The banker was so glad his banking friend's ranch was going to be saved that he was willing to do anything to help.

Chapter 13.

Clint was back at the poker table at the agreed time. The gambler was there ahead of Clint and had taken the chair in the corner facing the bar. Clint's trained eye also picked out the slight bulge at the gambler's waist that hadn't been there before. Clint took the seat to the gambler's right, which seemed to displease the man a whole lot. The eastern buyer was late, as expected of this overbearing, arrogant cattle buyer, but Clint waited with a deep down satisfaction. Pride, power and money were the chief building blocks of Mr. Jeffrey Lackston. By the end of this day and night, Clint was going to destroy this thief with far greater pain than a bullet.

During the next twelve hours almost a dozen card players moved in and out of this game, but three men never left the table except when a break was called by all for food and personal needs.

Clint had continued his gradual winning with more and larger pots as the day wore on. The gambler got more and more sullen and on a couple of occasions, Clint watched as the gambler's hand would adjust the object under his waistband just out of sight from the card players. Mr. Lackston continued to lose, but the occasional pot that came his way kept his spirits up.

During two breaks, the cattle buyer had returned to his room for cash and once Clint had seen him headed for the bank just before closing hours.

Clint was now entering the critical stage of this man-destroying game. He must keep the trigger-happy gambler from tearing the game apart before he had taken every cent the cattle buyer had. The prideful Mr. Lackston must be challenged on his pride so he would not let the amount of money being lost convince him to leave the game. Clint started letting the gambler win a few pots to keep him friendly. By about midnight, only five players were still at the table. Two other cattle buyers who knew Mr. Lackston had joined the table a couple of hours earlier. Clint had won rather heavily the last two hours. The heavy betting was aided by the other two cattle buyers who seemed to have a lot more money than card sense.

Clint could see that Lackston was running out of cash; his betting was getting slow and he was folding early on fairly good hands. Clint started setting the pride hooks by making statements like, "A real man, a true western man could beat any eastern businessman at cards." Clint slid several more comments in on Lackston about losing his nerve and if he didn't have money to play he should get out of this real man's game and go over and play the penny-ante poker with the green horns at the tables up front. Clint got the response he wanted. Jeff Lackston told the table if they really wanted to play cards the limits should be lifted, then they would see who the real man was in this group. Anyone who didn't have the stomach for this should pack their bags now. Jeff Lackston had been boasting how he had bought the best cattle in these parts for one half the going rate. He mentioned that the herd was at the loading docks awaiting the next train east. He would put up those cattle at his purchase price in lieu of money since he was temporarily out of cash until those cattle sold. The other cattle buyers quickly accepted the promissory notes on the cattle as cash because they knew a good deal when they saw one. The other buyers still had a lot of cash, because Lackston had somehow found these herds before they had gotten into town.

The new game rules opened the game up completely. The old bluffing tactic that Lackston loved to use came out in full force. Clint now had almost enough cash to start a bank. He was sure that with some exceptional skill on his part he could ride over any good hands that Jeff Lackston was lucky enough to draw. The one thing that greatly concerned Clint was the level of the gambler's cheating. As the stakes got higher, the gambler's true colors came out. Clint was afraid the cattle buyers would notice the dealing tricks and call the whole thing off.

Clint had picked up on the rough edges of the kings and aces; the kings were marked on the left and the aces on the right. Whoever was dealing the cards could feel these marked cards.

Clint waited until a hand when he had three queens and could tell that the gambler was going to deal himself the third king on the draw. To prevent a shootout and ruin the chance of cleaning out Mr. Lackston, Clint pulled his gun and pointing it straight at the gambler, called his hand. Clint turned up his hand showing three queens, then told the group what the gambler's next card would be—a king. The cattle buyers couldn't believe that this sleek card dealer had almost taken them. Clint offered a solution. All the gambler's winnings would be taken from him and put on the table. The winner of the next hand with new cards would take all. The gambler would get off with his life. Jeff Lackston's eyes looked as big as saucers when the gambler was stripped of all his possessions. In addition to the cash in his pockets, the gambler had a pearl-handled revolver stuck in a fat money belt. The money belt was packed full of gold pieces and other cash. The greedy cattle buyer was already counting those gold coins in his mind. You could see in his face how this eastern gent would be telling this tale about how he had stripped a tough, slick-as-grease, smooth gambler of all his money and run him out of the saloon with only the clothes on his back and his life.

As the gambler left the table, those steel-cold eyes gave Clint one last look full of hate. It was as if the gambler wanted to burn Clint's image into his mind.

The winner-take-all card game was going to be seven card stud with three cards down. Clint drew the deal with a new deck of cards. The first round gave Mr. Lackston a king and the other two cattle buyers a jack and a ten. Clint pulled a seven of hearts. Two cards were dealt down and the game was on. Clint could almost read the excitement in Lackston's eyes and face as he prepared to do in Clint and the other two on this one hand. Clint didn't often resort to working the cards with cheating, but it was now or never and the arrogant Lackston was going to get his just reward if Clint had his way.

Clint palmed a king and a jack in the second round, dealing himself a three of hearts plus an ace of clubs. Clint knew that Lackston had one king showing and one down, beating anything showing. Lackston bet on the king and raised twice, using his note on the cattle as collateral. The other buyers had agreed on a ten thousand dollar price tag for the cattle and Lackston had been betting on that money heavily for the past hour. Clint had figured pretty close that he could match all the money the eastern cattle buyer had with him including the remaining balance on the cattle I.O.U.

When the last card face up was dealt, Lackston bet one thousand dollars. Clint had given him his third king. The other two cattle buyers folded and left Clint holding, face up, two sevens and a total of three hearts with a possible inside straight or flush. Clint put on a good act of sweating the bet and he could tell that he had convinced Lackston of his upper hand. Clint reluctantly called but Lackston raised with another one thousand dollar bet trying to now buy the pot. By now the saloon crowd, what few were left at three a.m., had sensed the high stakes that were being played at the rear table. No one moved in too close, but a large half circle formed around the poker game as the excitement grew. The bartender set up a free round of drinks and spirits were boosted to a fever pitch. No one in this town had seen that much money, Clint even doubted the bank usually had that much cash on hand, other than when major mining payrolls were due.

With the last card played face down, it was Lackston's turn to bet his kings high. He put up a two thousand dollar note, the last remaining amount on his herd. Lackston thought he had Clint when Clint had run out of cash on the table to meet the bet. As Lackston leaned over the table to drag in the pot, Clint laid a firm, trail-hardened hand on top of those white soft hands and with a grip that put pain in the eyes of this arrogant cattle thief, Clint told him to hold on a minute. Clint then reached into the top of his boot and pulled out a small money pouch and carefully counted out his call bet. Lackston had thought he had bought the pot, but winning it with his three kings and two aces for a full house would give him even more satisfaction.

When Lackston laid out the ace high full house the whole crowd gave a deep moan. Most of these guys would have loved to see that quiet, slow spoken, but tough-playing cowboy walk away with this pot. He would have been able to buy almost any ranch in these parts with that kind of money. When Clint turned over his small straight heart flush, the saloon went wild. The onlookers gathered around Clint, slapping him on the back. Several guys went out into the street and were shooting off their guns. It almost seemed like the 4th of July. Clint watched a defeated Jeff Lackston almost shrink before his very eyes. Clint had been right—this defeat was far worse for the likes of this arrogant money manager than a quick bullet to the heart. Lackston would sneak out of town, never to be seen or heard of again. He was probably out here with a lot of other investors' money and probably could never return home again. He would be known in his eastern hometown as a thief and scoundrel.

Chapter 14.

By the time the party was over and Clint had bought everyone in the saloon all the drinks they could handle, it was almost midmorning the next day. Clint's back was as sore as if he had been whipped with a thorn bush. Everyone kept coming over to tell him how great a card game it had been and how lucky he was, and each time they felt a need to give him a hearty slap on the back. Clint let himself out the front door of the saloon just as he saw the banker, Mr. Jenson, opening up the bank. Clint had timed his departure with skill. He had not wanted to leave that saloon under the cover of night, but bright daylight, and he was headed straight across the street to the bank.

Clint told Mr. Jenson what had gone on last night and the good luck he had. Clint said he wanted to pay off the Big M debt and asked him to give him proof of the debt payoff. He was sure that Brad Mason would give him a job for life. The banker told Clint that would be better than the cash, because he would probably never be so lucky again. Mr. Jenson assured Clint that he was making a fine choice. The banker also was trying to get Clint to invest in the Jordan ranch. He knew that Clint could buy up the notes on that ranch with the cash and gold that he still had and with the cattle he had to sell down at the loading pens.

Clint acted reluctant with excuses that Alice and Ben Toss had given him a job when he needed one. It didn't seem right to buy out the ranch without their even knowing about it.

Jensen then suggested that he buy up the notes on the Circle J ranch but give the owner another year to make payment. Clint felt that was a good idea but asked that his name be kept out of it and put all the notes under Brad Mason's name. Jenson said that he would put out the world that Brad had found another investor from back east. Clint chuckled at this, for it was essentially true. Both men got a good laugh out of it when they thought about Lackston's money and cattle being Brad's investor.

Clint wanted a much-needed rest after all the night card playing and all morning partying, plus the business transactions. He did not want to hang around town so he hit the trail back toward Clifton and the Manatee Valley. He had been gone much too long. However, he slept well that afternoon and all the next night in a protected cave off the main trail.

Clint's first mission was completed. He had fleeced one of the buyers of stolen cattle and stopped the foreclosure on the Big M ranch. However, he knew that unless he could rout that band of gunslingers Ron had pulled together, the war could be lost even though he had won this major battle.

Clint's plan to seek out, one at a time, Ron's bandits and demoralize the gang was stopped cold when Clint rode into Clifton for supplies. He had only intended to briefly visit the dry goods store and get out of town. To his surprise the gambler was standing on the hotel veranda next to the Copper Nickel Saloon when Clint went by. The gambler immediately went back inside. Clint knew he had pulled a dumb thing by coming into this town. As he went into the dry goods store, he saw the gambler and Ron standing at the saloon door pointing in his direction. Clint quickly gathered a few things, including two extra boxes of cartridges for both Tom's rifle and his Colt 44 pistol. If Clint could get out of town before Ron had time to round up his gang, maybe he still had a chance. His horse was tired from the ride down from Santa Fe, but that roan stallion had lots of power and endurance.

Before Clint was over the first rise out of town, he saw Ron and at least six other riders mount up and take out after him. Clint knew he needed to get at least a mile between him and those gun toters because some of them were no doubt good rifle shots. Clint was within one hundred yards of the next crest when bullets started kicking up dust all around him. Ron, like a well-trained general, had had his two best rifle shots dismount and start firing at Clint while the rest of the gang came on strong.

Just when Clint thought he was going to make it he felt the sharp burning in his side. He held onto the saddle horn as his horse carried him over the crest in the road. He felt the roan miss its footing, then get its balance and charge on down the road out of sight of the guns.

Clint knew he was losing blood fast and if he didn't stop the bleeding he would lose his strength to stay in the saddle. He gave the roan his head for a flat out run to get as much distance between him and Ron as possible. Clint had never called on this horse like he was now. It was a do or die run. The roan was over the next hill before Ron's men ever came into sight. Two more hills were taken at break neck speed. The roan was running his heart out with Clint sort of floating in the saddle. Up ahead, Clint saw a rock outcrop that extended out both sides of the road and right up to scrub oak cover on both sides. When the roan got onto the rock surface Clint carefully slowed him so no marks would be made. Then the two of them slipped off into the scrub oak trees and waited. Clint bandaged himself as tight as he could stand it. The bullet had gone in at his lower back near the left side and hade come out the front leaving a terrible hole. It didn't feel like any ribs were broken, but he felt the fire burning inside. Clint knew that even if he could stop the outside bleeding by applying pressure, he would probably still be bleeding inside.

Ron's gang had ridden on by and a few minutes later the two long shooters passed by trying to catch up so they could be in on the kill. After a few minutes Clint mounted and by tying this belt to the saddle horn, he hoped to stay in the saddle as he gave the roan free rein to take him to safety.

Chapter 15.

Clint didn't know how long he had been out when he realized the roan was no longer moving. It was still dark but a little light was starting to form in the sky. Clint then saw that the roan had brought him to the Circle J north range cabin that had been their home all summer. The sorrel mare was standing next to the roan, probably glad to see them after all this time.

Clint unhooked his belt from the saddle horn and slid to the ground. He was expecting to fall flat on his face, but his legs held. His bleeding must have stopped, for he had seen other guys bleed to death in less time. Moving as carefully as possible, Clint walked the roan over to some bushes and unhooked his saddle, letting it fall to the ground. He then took off the bridle and let the roan go. Making sure he did not stretch his body, he made up some cold oatmeal and water. With a canteen full of water and blankets, he made his way out of the cabin and back into the thick underbrush. He ate and drank in small bites then drifted off to sleep for a short while. This went on all day, but by late afternoon Clint's head was beginning to clear a little.

Just about sunset Ron and six men rode up to the cabin. Clint could hear them cussing and arguing about how he could have disappeared. The tall, lean looking one that Clint had seen on the cattle-stealing job off the Circle J kept saying that he knew he had hit the rider or the horse. After ransacking the cabin the bunch rode north, except Ron. Clint overheard him say that he was going down to the ranch and report to Hudson. This confirmation of Clint's suspicions was welcome as he settled into another deep sleep.

He woke just before daylight and could hardly move his whole midsection. It was either the pain or Clint was better because his mind was clear. He could think about what needed to be done, whereas yesterday all he could think about was his pain and bleeding to death.

After a few tries, Clint was able to get up without tearing open the wound; he wasn't sure what was going on inside his body. He went into the cabin and cleaned the wound and redressed it with some iodine and clean cloth.

The cabin was a mess after that crew of Ron's had been through it, but Clint had stocked it pretty well the last three months. Clint was careful not to leave any traces of his presence. He picked up selected items from the cabin that he would need for the next week or two. Clint knew it would take at least a week at best before he could be active again and that would be only if infection didn't set in. If that did occur, he would probably die out there in the bush. No one would know what had become of the lucky cowboy who had won a fortune in Santa Fe from a rich, arrogant, eastern cattle buyer.

A deep down feeling of satisfaction swept through Clint. He knew that if he never did another thing he had finally helped his brother, even if five years late. He had also won the biggest card game he had ever heard about. He knew a lot of good men that couldn't beat that if they lived to be eighty years old.

Clint went out to get the horses and for the first time saw that the roan had been badly hurt in the escape. A slug had cut a deep slice right into the hindquarter muscle. Clint marveled again at the strength and endurance of that big roan stallion. That horse had carried him at top speed after he was hit and had then carried his wounded rider over rugged country to this cabin. Clint went back into the cabin and found the ointment he kept around for animal injuries. He bathed the wound and treated it to prevent infection. The roan seemed to know that he was in good hands.

It took Clint several tries to get the saddle out of the bushes where he had dropped it off and up on the sorrel mare's back. He could not strain too much and take a chance on opening his wounds. However, he had to get away from here if he was to recoup. He knew that Ron would keep looking for the cowboy that always seemed to be in the right place at the wrong time.

Chapter 16.

Clint walked the first mile or so leading the mare. This gave him a chance to limber up and to cover their tracks well. By traveling a few hours at a time, it took almost two days to reach his hideaway. The cave home had not been disturbed and all the supplies he had stowed there were still in good shape.

Clint unsaddled the mare and turned her loose. The roan had trailed them so Clint took some extra time to care for its wound. It looked really bad, but the stallion seemed to be walking okay. Clint was dead tired and his stomach wound was red hot. He could tell his temperature would flare up, then go down for a couple of hours, then flare up again. He had no way of knowing how bad his gunshot wound was, but he couldn't go into Crossbow to see the doctor. He kept up the self-treatment of keeping the wound clean, drinking as much water as he could, along with frequent small, soft food meals. He was so burned out on oatmeal that he could spit, but he continued the diet.

He had remembered a gut shot man in Crossbow when he was a small boy that the doctor had treated this way. Everyone in the community had always said that if you got gut shot it was all over, except for a slow painful death. The doctor had pulled the fellow through with water and oatmeal. Clint remembered how the doctor had warned the guy not to eat any solid food for three weeks. During the second week when the man thought he was healing good and he felt pretty well, he sneaked a steak. You could hear the guy screaming for a whole block with stomach pain. Clint made up his mind that he would give himself a month even if he could never eat oatmeal and mush again.

The next week was really bad for Clint. His fever would go up and down, then he would break out in a cold sweat and soak his bedding. However, by the end of that week he knew he was going to make it. It would take two or three more weeks to get his strength back. He doubted that he would really feel very well until he could eat a good meal of steak and potatoes.

He lay there day after day wondering what was going on in the valley. He was afraid that Captain Hudson would turn Ron's gang loose on the valley ranchers if he didn't get his hands on at least the Circle J. He was also worried that the outlaws might try to get Brad into some kind of situation so they could legally kill him or get him off the Big M.

Clint, with complete self-discipline, held himself to his treatment plan. He knew if he died it would only help the enemy. He was too close to helping his brother to lose now. Each day Clint gradually increased his exercise, being careful not to tear open his wounds. His strength returned rapidly the second week, but he knew that overconfidence was a real threat.

During the third and fourth week he was starting to almost feel like himself. He was running short of ammunition due to his daily practice with pistol and rifle. He was going to have to make a trip into Morristown the next weekend. He needed to start the last phase of the plan, but he needed information on what was going on in Crossbow. If he was to carry out his plan, he must avoid being recognized by any of Ron's gang. No doubt the good trackers in Ron's gang probably had found where he had gone off the trail and all the blood Clint had spilled while waiting undercover. Let them think the cowboy they knew as Cliff Martin had died, or else let them think he ran for his life and left the country.

Chapter 17.

Clint set out early Friday morning, almost five weeks after he had been shot. He felt good on this crisp fall morning. The cottonwoods were just starting to turn a golden tinge. In another month, the canyon slopes off in the distance would be golden yellow, almost too bright to look at in a midday sun. Freedom from his cave hideout also served to boost his spirits. The roan he was riding had healed as quickly as himself and Clint could tell the horse wanted to get on with their task.

Clint got into Morristown late and went straight to the steak house where he had eaten last spring. He ate very cautiously and with a little fear, since this was his first major meal in over a month. The food seemed to agree with him as he could almost feel the strength from that juicy steak flow into his muscles. His self-treatment was a real success and he felt like it was time to get on with this operation.

Clint was able to get into a friendly card game at the Golden Coin Saloon as some of the ranch cowboys were starting to arrive for their monthly weekend. In fact, Clint recognized two of the ranch hands he had played with last spring during his first visit to Morristown. They immediately recognized him and came over to his table. They remembered the good weekend they had spent together and the fact that this fellow player had left town with money after playing cards for two days solid.

The table conversation started almost immediately with what had been going on in the valley all summer. When Clint let them know that he had been up north all summer out of the county, they felt compelled to fill him in on all the news.

Brad Mason had found an outside investor and had held off Captain Hudson's foreclosure. The Captain had made a public show of how happy he was that Brad had found someone to help him. Most of the cowboys at the table didn't buy this public display from Captain Hudson for one minute. They were betting that Hudson was mad enough to have had a fit when word came down from the Santa Fe bank that the Big M had obtained new financing.

The biggest story of all was the closure of Circle J ranch. A gang of outlaws had raided the ranch's biggest herd and killed four of the wranglers. However, the Circle J crew had managed to kill four of the outlaws. When the sheriff had investigated the identity and background of the dead outlaws, he found that two of them had been wanted, dead or alive. Alice Jordan had been given a one thousand dollar reward for her crew killing those outlaws. However, without ranch hands and her best herd driven off, she had turned her ranch over to Captain Hudson to manage. Ben Toss had gone to work for Brad Mason with Alice Jordan's blessing.

Captain Hudson had won Alice's attention by wining and dining her like a princess. Everyone could understand why she had agreed to wed the ever-popular Carl Hudson. He was the best-dressed gentleman in the whole region, his ranch house was the finest in the county, and he had the crew and money to put the Circle J back on its feet. The combined two ranches would be the largest in the county, except for the Big M. A fall wedding had been planned, right after fall roundup. Alice had insisted that she pay off all her debts with a complete roundup of her cattle before she got married. Ben Toss had reminded Alice of the sizeable herd in the northern range in excellent condition that Cliff Martin had tended prior to the raid. Ben had told Alice that the herd would be a good start on rebuilding the Circle J, but Alice had had enough, she would sell them and pay off all friends who had helped her since her dad and brother had gotten killed. Several of the merchants in Crossbow had carried accounts for the ranch for several years. She was an honest and loyal neighbor and was going to pay them back if it took her last cent.

The other news was that Ben Toss had also found a sizeable herd of Big M cattle on the northern range of the Circle J. Alice had insisted that all those cattle be returned to Brad Mason's ranch. While the cattle were being rounded up, a large number of Big M horses were found. The strangest thing about that herd of horses was a big black stallion with a fairly fresh Big M brand. Some of the crew from the Captain H Ranch that was helping Alice Jordan clear up her affairs let it be known that the big stallion looked just like the one the missing gunslinger Tom rode. But Alice Jordan insisted that all the horses and cattle with the Big M brand be turned over to Brad Mason.

The cowboys around the card table at the Golden Coin were saying that Brad Mason would be in a good position come next spring to rebuild the Big M with the return of all his horses and cattle that had been found on the northern section of the Circle J. The cowboys who had rounded up the herd off Circle J, under the close eye of Alice Jordan, had found the best breeding bull ever seen in these parts. Alice had personally seen to it that the breeding bull was turned over to Brad. Something mysterious had been happening to the bulls on the range in Manatee County, so Alice did not take any chances letting that bull out of her sight until she turned it over to Brad personally.

Ben Toss, upon joining the Big M, had taken special care to make sure his new boss didn't lose that bull. Ben Toss had told several of the cowboys the last time he was in town that the Big M should have the largest calf crop this coming spring they had seen in over five years.

The cowboys also reported that they no longer went to Clifton, since the gunman Ron Johnson just about ruled the town. It always worked out to be self-defense, but Ron had gunned down more Manatee County ranchers and cowboys than anyone wanted to count. Even since his sidekick Tom had disappeared, Ron had gotten meaner than a snake. It was also reported that several of the heavily armed men that Ron often hung-out with had not been seen in Clifton for weeks and two or three rough-looking gents were hanging around with bandages. These wounded gentlemen seemed to have shown up right after Tom's reported disappearance and the raid on the Circle J ranch.

What Clint couldn't understand was why someone in Manatee County had not connected Ron and his gunmen, the raids on valley cattle and Captain Hudson all together as the underlying cause for the demise of so many ranches. Clint hadn't seen this Hudson for ten years, but he must be quite a gentleman if he could keep in the good graces of the valley people with so much circumstantial evidence against him.

Clint could only remember the look in Hudson's eyes when, as a little wiry boy, Clint had out-shot him at the Manatee County annual get together. If looks could have killed, Clint would never have made it to manhood. However, Clint did remember the ever-proper Captain Hudson had put on a good show of good sportsmanship by praising the young lad when someone of importance was around.

Clint now wondered if Hudson, by some method, had worked behind the scenes to get Clint chased out of town with the threat of death if he was caught. Whoever had built the frame against Clint had been good. Not only did it get rid of Clint, but it probably put a black eye on the whole Mason ranch, which Brad no doubt had to live down.

Clint had promised himself that he would never embarrass Brad or the Mason name again and thus would never let himself be caught in Manatee County.

Clint had gone by the name of Cliff Martin whenever he was forced to give a name. Most of the time the initials C.M. were enough of a handle. The only one who had ever used the title on Clint was his older brother, Brad. Brad always told Clint that initials as a call name seemed right for Clint. It was one of those rare, close bonds between brothers that no one could ever come between, not even when circumstances put miles of distance between them. Clint had come to Brad's aid the first moment he heard the call for help. The risk to Clint's life was not even considered when the question was asked, can you help.

Chapter 18.

Clint was enjoying the open conversation over the friendly poker games, but good times have a way of suddenly turning into bad times. Clint had just won a small pot on three Jacks when out of the corner of his eye he caught a glimpse of the gambler who had identified him for Ron and had almost gotten him killed. As soon as the gambler saw Clint, he left the saloon in almost a run.

Clint very lazily dismissed himself and went out the back door as if going to the outhouse. His ears had told him that the gambler had turned north up the street so Clint moved north up the alley. He could hear the rapid footsteps on the boardwalk just a block ahead of him. Clint ran without a sound on the fine powdery sand in the alley. Clint reached the end of the second block at the same time the gambler stepped off the boardwalk. Clint waited to see if the gambler would turn or keep going on down Main Street. The gambler turned away from where Clint was and headed up the opposite direction toward the livery stable.

By the time Clint had worked his way across Main Street without being seen and started to enter the stable, the gambler had saddled up inside and was riding out. The gambler wasn't expecting to see Clint there in front of him and he pulled back on the reins hard just as the horse was coming through the doorway. The horse reared up both from being spooked by Clint and by the hard pull on the reins by the gambler.

The sickening thud that Clint heard was the complete story. The gambler's head had been crushed by the impact of the barn door's crossbeam as he was driven upward by the full force of the rearing horse. The gambler never knew what hit him. Clint looked around and found that the attendant or stable boy was nowhere to be seen. Clint carefully covered up his boot tracks and returned to the poker table as calm as a man who had just heeded nature's call and was returning to his place at the table. It was almost an hour later when someone came into the saloon and reported that the gambler had mounted his horse in the stable and had gotten his head smashed when the horse had either bucked or reared up as they came through the stable door.

The cowboys talked about the gambler and his close association with Ron Johnson. Most of them had wished the gambler had stayed up in Clifton with the rest of his friends. It was felt that Ron and his gunmen might come down to Morristown when they heard of the gambler's accidental death. Ron had been on the prod for weeks and just looked for excuses to push his weight around. The poker game soon broke up with the cowboys deciding they had had enough and were heading back to their ranches before Ron showed up.

Clint moved out of town with the rest of the cowboys with no one the wiser. Everyone headed off in his own direction without a word, thus Clint never had to give any information on his plans or whereabouts.

Chapter 19.

Clint felt now was the time. The big roan stallion was in pretty good shape and Clint felt as if he was also as ready as he was going to get. The task at hand was to try and catch one or two of the rustlers isolated so Clint could convince them with a few good shots, that they didn't want to play the Manatee County game that Captain Hudson and Ron Johnson had dealt them into. Clint decided that Ron would probably bring several of his boys into Morristown in a few days to follow-up on the accident that had taken his gambling friend's life. Ron was losing too many associates not to be a little spooked by this death. However, Ron would leave a few behind in Clifton, so Clint's plan was to watch Clifton when Ron left and try to catch some of the boys asleep on the job.

Clint had been watching Clifton with his spyglass for two days before the word got to Ron. He took five men and headed south at a fast pace. Ron had not been gone four hours when Clint spotted the long, lean gun handler who had taken credit for the rifle shot into Clint. The tall one rode at a very quick pace, almost right toward Clint. He passed just below Clint by crossing over the saddle of the ridge and continued down a small trail.

This was the kind of break that Clint wanted so he stayed on the gunman's trail until they were several miles out of town. Clint then let himself be seen, knowing the tall one would have to investigate. Clint kept his hat pulled down low so his face couldn't be seen and rode right up to where he had seen the other guy pull his horse off the trail. Clint was expecting a challenge and even though the tall, thin sharpshooter had his gun out, Clint drew and fired before he did. The rider fired only one shot that went into the ground as he fell. Clint made a search of the body then unsaddled the horse and turned it loose. Clint rode on down the trail trying to find out where this rider was headed as soon as Ron had left town. Just a few miles down the trail was a run-down range shack. After watching it for a while, Clint decided that the tall one must have had a woman out here, but that Ron didn't approve, so he had to sneak out when Ron was out of town.

Clint decided to watch the trail again to see if someone would come out to check on the tall one. So Clint rounded up the dead man's horse and resaddled it. Then, by taking the horse back over the trail down through the saddle toward town, Clint thought the horse would return to the Clifton stable.

Clint got back into a good position to watch the town. After the horse's return to Clifton, it didn't take long for the stable boy to identify the horse and report to someone in the Copper Nickel Saloon. Within a few minutes two gents came out and went straight to the stable. Two mounted riders rode out of the barn and straight up the same trail, so they must have known where the tall sharpshooter spent some of his off hours. Clint moved back down the trail to a good spot he had seen a little earlier. The scrub oak was thick and almost grew right up to the trail. Clint waited until the two bandits were within fifty feet, stepped out into the trail directly in front of them and drew his gun. Both men stopped their horses in complete surprise, never expecting a lone gunman on foot to confront them. Clint had sized them up through his spyglass. Both of them had been in on the raid of the Circle J, but the one on the left had to be taken out first.

Clint got a quick shot into the tough looking rascal on the left just as his gun was clearing the holster, then another shot into the upper body of the slower gent on the right. The blow knocked him right out of the saddle. The tough guy on the right fired on Clint but missed and Clint drilled him dead center. As he was disarming the two, Clint saw that the slower gunman was still alive, but his shooting shoulder was ruined for life. The other guy was dead before he hit the ground.

Clint then removed all their holsters, guns, rifles and any valuables they had, except for a few dollars he left for the injured, but unconscious rustler. The next step was even smart for Clint. He went back and got the body of the tall gunman and loaded both dead bodies on one horse and the unconscious guy on the other horse and headed down the road to the shack where the lady friend lived.

Clint kept his bandanna over his face and told the woman that this was only the beginning of the trouble that would befall anyone who raided the ranchers of Manatee County. He was only a messenger of the vigilante group that had dealt Ron's gang a serious blow starting with Tom's group and the warning on the raid against Circle J. Now they were going to get each one of the twelve raiders who had taken part in the Circle J ranch raid, of which six had already been killed and at least two were wounded. Clint told her to fix the one guy up so he could ride and if he got out of the country, at least he would have his life.

Clint then rode off in the direction away from Clifton. He knew that there could only be a few of the gang left in town, probably only two or three. After confusing his tracks, he headed back to Clifton to put some extra fear into the gang.

Chapter 20.

Clint went straight to the local gun shop, which was part of the dry goods store, and put all the outlaws' shooting hardware on the counter. Clint could tell the gunsmith and storekeeper recognized some of the equipment, but Clint demanded a fair price for the guns and holsters and was paid quickly. The fear on the gunsmith's face told Clint he had done the right thing, bringing that hardware right back into their home territory. This was either going to blow the valley wide apart or cause the gang to disintegrate. If Ron could hold his group together after this, Clint would be amazed.

Hopefully, Ron would have to openly join Captain Hudson and use the Captain H Ranch crews to carry out any more dirty work. This would then discredit Captain Hudson. If he got control of the Circle J, maybe he didn't care if his cover was blown. Clint had lost some track of time, but he knew by the chill in the air that fall roundup was close and that meant the Jordan/Hudson wedding was near.

Clint asked the gunsmith where the best saloon was for a good hand of poker. As Clint had thought, he was directed to the older saloon down the street rather than to the Copper Nickel where Ron's men would be hanging out, if any were in town. Clint moved slowly down the street to the saloon that had been pointed out to him, but kept a close eye on the gunsmith shop. As soon as Clint turned into the dark doorway of the saloon he saw the gunsmith head out to the Copper Nickel. Not ten minutes had passed when three gents with fire in their steps came out of the Copper Nickel Saloon and rode south out of town without looking back.

Clint knew that he had thrown the challenge squarely into Ron Johnson's face and if those riders hadn't decided to head out of the county, Ron should have the message from Clifton about his three men's guns. It would be assumed that all three had been killed, since their guns and holsters had been brought in and sold. Even at top speed, if those three riders didn't kill their horses, it would be at least two, maybe three days, before Ron could get the word and get back to Clifton, unless he had not stayed in Morristown.

Clint decided to move over near the Captain H Ranch and try to get an estimate of Hudson's strength. Also, he wanted to see what preparations were being made for fall roundup. No one in Clifton was talking to Clint now. Either everyone was afraid or, more likely, this was Ron Johnson's town and even the ones who didn't like him did not want to take the chance of making him mad by being seen with Clint. This tough looking cowboy had brought in three sets of hardware from Ron's men and had the nerve to sell them to the local gun dealer. It was not unusual to buy and sell used guns. The men in the west did a lot of trading, especially if they needed money or had some extra funds. But, Clint had also put Tom's rifle on his horse. That gun was so rare and expensive that few others had ever been seen. Just as Clint headed out of Clifton, he saw the lady from the shack ride into town and go into the Copper Nickel Saloon. If her story didn't put Ron in direct contact with Captain Hudson, then Clint had missed in his assessment of this whole situation.

Clint stopped off at the Circle J north range cabin to see what supplies he could round up. He also decided to straighten the place up again so it would give Ron and his men just another piece to think about. He arranged the table and dishes to look like at least six men had stopped there for a break. He rode his horse all around the cabin several times and marked up the area as if a lot of traffic had been in and out. He got a good night's sleep with the roan standing guard and was off to the Captain H Ranch before daylight.

Clint took three days to scout the Hudson range and watch the main house, but saw no unusual activity. It was beginning to look as though his theory might be wrong.

On the fourth day Clint spotted a sizeable herd being moved into a holding area just a few miles south of the main ranch house. Now Clint realized that Captain Hudson had decided to speed up the roundup. He had put all his men to getting that task done rather than chasing an elusive gunman who was playing havoc with Ron's men.

Clint moved in as close as possible, but could not recognize any of the cowhands. Ron was not in the group, so his plan to cause the open display of Ron working with Captain Hudson had not worked. Something had gone wrong and time was running out. The wedding would be any day now.

Clint decided to try to sneak into Crossbow to find out what was going on. However, after traveling about half way he changed his mind. If he got caught and identified, all his efforts to help Brad would have been wasted. He would probably be lynched for all the killing and rustling that had been going on. It could also be reworked by Hudson to look as if Clint and Brad, being brothers, had worked together to kill off the Captain H Ranch cowboys and take over the whole valley. Clint had gotten a huge amount of money and paid off the Big M ranch debts, purchased the notes on the Circle J and had them put into Brad Mason's name.

The more Clint thought about it, the more frightened he became. If Hudson had figured out his identity, everything he had done could be turned to work against Brad. It could be used to not only ruin Brad's lifelong developed reputation, but also take away his ranch and home. It could also get Brad hung as an accessory to the crime and killings.

A cold sweat broker out all over Clint as this idea played through his head. He had always prided himself in being a pretty smart guy, but the plan he had so carefully carried out could destroy Brad and himself. He mentally lashed himself for not having seen the potential problems and high risk his game plan had created.

Chapter 21.

Clint rode back into Morristown a defeated man in his own mind. His only goal had been to help his brother in his time of need, but now the world seemed to be on the brink of falling in on his brother and himself.

He was deep in thought as he rode into Morristown and put his horse in the commercial stable at the edge of town. As he dismounted he heard the click of a single action pistol being cocked. Without a pause, his mind, with years of conditioning, took over and put his body in motion. His action was similar to what Tom's had been that day when Clint had almost bought it. Clint's first shot, as he hit the ground, was dead center where the sound had come from and one back-shooter was down for good. Two more guns roared as they aimed toward the point from where Clint had first fired. It was so dark in the stable that only the blinding flashes of the firing guns could be seen. Clint fired again from another position as he rolled and fired in one motion. The second thud and groan let the world know that a man was leaving this earthly state.

All was still except Clint's rapid heartbeat. He was sure the third gunman could hear it and Clint lay perfectly still, just waiting for a bullet to tear into his body. Off to his left, he heard the slight noise of footsteps on straw. If he fired and missed, the gunman could hit him easily. Even rolling left his whole body would be exposed, for the sound was almost right beside him, not twenty feet away. Clint knew that the wooden stalls were very close and the man could be protected behind their thick walls.

The horses were now stomping around, trying to get away from all the noise and the smells of blood and gunpowder. It seemed as if time was taking forever, but Clint's steel will kept him absolutely still. He now knew that the other gunman didn't know where he was or if he was still alive, but he wasn't going to take a chance. It seemed like hours even though it had been only minutes and seconds.

Noises were starting to come from the street outside. All the shooting had awakened half the town, but no one seemed brave enough to venture into the stable. Someone outside said they had seen Ron Johnson go into the stable earlier tonight, but didn't know what all the shooting was about. Clint now knew his adversary was the top gunman himself.

Ron's voice came from out of the darkness, farther back to Clint's left and very soft, but clear. He called out, "Clint Mason, I know that is you." Captain Hudson had figured out that the only man alive who would have some reason to meddle in Manatee County business and who could shoot that well was Brad Mason's brother. Ron said, "I have heard about you for ten years from Carl and I am sick and tired of it. I've always wondered if you were really as fast and accurate as Carl remembered. I've always wanted to meet you and when I described you to Carl after our card game in Clifton, he was pretty sure it was you. Then when all the trouble started, he was convinced that you had returned to help your brother save the old homestead. The only man in this whole region that I ever thought could be a close match for me was Captain Carl Hudson. He looks like a southern gentleman without a rough edge anywhere, but under that cover is pure devil. I rode with him in Missouri and Kansas before he decided to come here and start a respectable life with a title and all its trappings. I'm telling you all of this because you have always been a big mystery to me and only a storybook figure in tales told by Carl. I must know whether you're as good as he says you are or has Carl just built you up as a legend in his own mind. I will tell you that the Captain got a real laugh out of how he framed you and sent you packing without a fight. However, he always said he regrets not doing you in himself after your lucky shooting that embarrassed him in front of the town folks of Crossbow that he was trying so hard to impress.

"Let's call a truce and meet two miles south of town at first light in the morning. There is a big oak tree out in the open about one hundred feet off the road and right next to a big ox bow in the river. I must know which of us is the best. If you don't show, Captain Hudson is going to break your brother as soon as the wedding is over next Sunday."

With that Clint heard the straw rustle again and a side door creak as Ron disappeared into the night. Clint scrambled for the loft and hid in the hay.

Shortly, someone outside said they heard someone riding out of town so the fight must be over. Clint heard several people come into the stable below and found the two gunmen dead. They were identified as two of the guys who had ridden into town a few days ago with Ron Johnson.

Chapter 22.

The town's people argued about what had gone on in the stable, with several thinking that the two men had killed each other. They thought the two had probably been arguing over their gambling winnings because the men who had ridden into town with Ron had all seemed in bad tempers. Also, when three more of Ron's crew had showed just a couple days ago, there had been a lot of arguing between the whole group. In fact, most of the town's people had been rather afraid that Ron might be moving his crew down to Morristown. They could see him taking over just like he had down in Clifton. But in the last few days after three new men had come tearing into town, it seemed that Ron's group kept getting smaller each day, as if they were leaving town one at a time when nobody was watching. In fact, the only three the town's people had seen all day had been these two, who must have killed each other, and Ron. Maybe Ron had also been involved in this shootout. There had been heated arguments between the three of them today at the back table of the saloon.

No one seemed to notice Clint's horse. After the doctor had come over and pronounced the two gunmen dead, Clint heard several people removing the bodies.

Clint stayed where he was until almost daylight then sneaked down to his roan stallion and headed south out of town.

Clint kept his guard up for an ambush, but was sure that Ron was sincere about wanting to meet him face to face in a fair gunfight. Clint could understand how a gunman like Ron would be bothered by Carl Hudson's continual relaying of a story about a boy wonder with guns. It would eat at his very soul until he knew who was best. Clint didn't have that need, but how else could he proceed? If Hudson was going to destroy Brad anyway, he had to try to take Ron now.

Clint knew that Ron was good and he did not deceive himself into thinking of anything beyond their meeting. For him there might not be a future after his meeting with Ron under that big oak tree that he could just make out up ahead in the early predawn light.

Ron's horse was tied nearby and he stood there like a giant statue ready to fight a charging, mystical army. Clint dismounted not over one hundred feet from where Ron was standing, dropped the reins of the roan and moved to one side so the horse was not in the line of fire. Without a word between them, they walked to within fifty feet of each other and stopped. As if a magic signal had been given that both men heard at the same time, both went for their side arms at once. Four shots rang out into the early morning, chilly, clear air so close together that the shots seemed as one prolonged roar. As the gunpowder smoke drifted off the scene, the silhouette of a lone, tall, muscular man stood looking down at the fallen challenger. The tall

95

man turned and mounted the roan and rode off northward.

Clint always felt a little sick after he was a part of taking another human's life, even though he had always done it through his own sense of justice or in self-defense. But his feeling of sickness was felt deep inside as he rode north to face Hudson. After hearing Ron's description of Carl Hudson, Clint knew that he may not win a face off with the smooth looking, deceptive Captain Hudson, but he must try. Clint had been no faster than Ron, but where Clint's first shot had hit its mark, Ron's had hit the ground not more than a foot in front of Clint. Ron's first shot had been pulled off too quickly, and before he could get the second shot off, Clint's first slug had knocked him off balance so his second shot went wild. Clint's second shot had sealed Ron's fate and his world went black.

Chapter 23.

Clint decided to return to visit his cave home/hideout before seeking out Captain Hudson. His weeks of living there while he had recovered from his wounds had given him the feeling of a home. The two horses seemed to accept the place as theirs as well. Clint spotted the mare grazing down the slope some distance from the cave hideaway. The mare raced over to join them just like a dog running to his master when the master returns home after a long absence.

Clint patted the mare's head and neck as the two horses got reacquainted. As Clint rode on up to the cave entrance he was unsuspecting of any trouble at this safe hiding place, but when the sorrel mare stopped short, put her ears forward and flared her nostrils, Clint dived out of the saddle just as a rifle shot rang out from the entrance to the hideout. Clint fanned his pistol toward the opening, firing as rapidly as the hammer could fall on the shells. Six shots were put into the opening from where the rifle shot had come. Clint then reached for his horse to retrieve his rifle, afraid each step would be his last as his muscles waited tensely for the impact of a rifle slug that never came.

Clint grabbed the beautiful rifle that Tom Townsend had so reluctantly left him, in what seemed like years ago and dove behind the closest large boulder he could find and waited. The time went by as if the hourglass had fallen on its side. The sun was starting to rise to midday and it was warm on Clint's back as he lay on the cold, damp ground. He finally called out for whoever was in the cave to give up or he was going to start ricocheting bullets into the entrance of the cave. Rifle slug fragments could tear a man to shreds bouncing around inside that rock opening at this close angle. Still no sound, so Clint sent two shots into the cave and he could hear the multiple hits of the slug go from one wall to the other, but still no response. After a few more shots, Clint edged out from his cover and moved up to the entrance. To his surprise, there lay Captain Hudson in a very dressy tan outfit lying flat on his back as if asleep, but a big deep red blotch was showing on his collar and shirt. Upon examining the body, Clint could see that one of his slugs had hit Hudson's rifle and like a slice of flattened steel had ricocheted off the rifle and sliced through his throat and neck. It had broken his neck and he had died instantly. Clint had been waiting for the deadly firepower to be returned while all that time, the handsome Captain Hudson had passed on into the next life.

Clint went through the dead man's pockets and found a note in his brother's handwriting. His brother had figured out who he was by a note from the Santa Fe banker that contained the initials C.M. Brad had finally remembered this cave hideout that he and Clint had found as boys. His note continued to express his gratitude for Clint's coming to his help and the great relief that he had felt when he had seen the initials C.M. Brad had thought that his brother was dead or had never received his letters of five years ago. Brad then told of his loss of his wife a few days ago when they were ambushed on the way out to the ranch. No one had been able to find out who had done it. Brad felt that the group of gunmen that hung around Clifton were his best bet, but he had no way to prove it. Ever since Ron Johnson had come into these parts there had been a string of problems and killings. Brad knew that Clint was the only person he could turn to for help to save the family ranch. Brad reminded Clint that the ranch was still half his. He went on to write that he knew Clint couldn't be seen in Crossbow, but he would always love him for being a brother in such a time of need.

Alice Jordan had postponed the wedding when Brad's wife had been killed and had turned out to be a very good friend and neighbor in his hour of suffering. Captain Hudson, Alice's fiancé, had gotten quite upset about Alice's decision to delay the wedding, but he was sure Alice and Carl Hudson would still be married—probably early next spring. Brad wrote that he would cancel the notes of debt that Clint had bought up on the Circle J as a wedding gift for Alice. She was the most caring and honest person he had ever seen and she was devoted to her ranch. Brad was sure if Clint had gotten to know Alice as he had, he would agree with him on this decision.

As Clint read the long letter over and over, a deep feeling of satisfaction settled over him. He had been called by his brother for help and he had responded.

As Clint rode off over the ridge away from Manatee County, the bond between the two brothers was strengthened again for life, even if they never had a chance to see each other face to face.

The deep feeling brought tears to his eyes as Clint, the roan stallion and the sorrel mare rode off into the sunset to seek their own life and a new name. The Cliff Martin name would have to be left in the sealed-off cave with the buried body of Captain Carl Hudson.

Clint's sadness for Brad over the loss of his wife would stay with him for a long time. In some way, his presence had brought that sorrow to his brother.

Clint had no way of knowing that within a little more than a year, the friendship that had developed between his brother and his neighbor would blossom into a beautiful love that each had never known to exist. Alice would give children to Brad that his first wife had been unable to provide. The combined ranches of the Circle J and the Big M would become known as the Circle J-M ranch with the best beef and horses in the southern part of New Mexico.

If Clint had been able to see only a small piece of Brad's future, he could have also shared in the tremendous love and appreciation that Brad felt toward him as the years moved on.

Would the future ever allow these brothers to meet again?

About the Author

William F. Martin was born on a Kentucky farm and moved west in the mid-sixties on an assignment with the federal government's program to help Native Americans. His assignment to Santa Fe, New Mexico, began a lifetime love affair with the American West. His writing interest was developed with the publishing of many technical journal articles and textbooks on environmental and engineering issues. He has given numerous papers and speeches, both domestically and internationally.

After assignments in South Dakota, Arizona, and Texas, he has lived near the Gulf of Mexico on Treasure Island, Florida, and in the Blue Ridge Mountains in Boone, North Carolina.